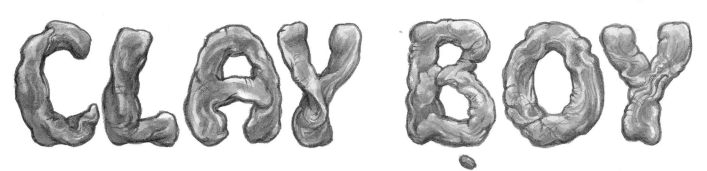

CLAY BOY

Adapted from a Russian Folk Tale
by **Mirra Ginsburg**

pictures by
Jos. A. Smith

Greenwillow Books, New York

The theme of *Clay Boy* appears in
the folklore of many countries, with a variety of plots
and details. This version was freely developed from
Russian sources.

—M. G.

Aquarelle and gouache paints were used for the
full-color art. The text type is Garamond ITC.

Manufactured in China.
First Edition   10

Library of Congress Cataloging-in-Publication Data

Ginsburg, Mirra.
Clay boy / adapted from a Russian folk tale by Mirra
Ginsburg ; pictures by Jos. A. Smith.
    p.   cm.
Summary: Wanting a son, an old man and woman
make a clay boy who comes to life and begins eating
everything in sight until he meets a clever goat.
ISBN 0-688-14409-8 (trade)
ISBN 0-688-14410-1 (lib. bdg.)
[1. Folklore—Russia.]
I. Smith, Joseph A. (Joseph Anthony), (date) ill.
II. Title.   PZ8.1.G455Cl   1997
398.2'0947'01—dc20
96-33820   CIP   AC

For Susan and Libby, with affection
—M. G.

For Charissa
—J. A. S.

In the village where I was born, there lived, a long, long time ago, an old man and an old woman— Grandpa and Grandma.

One day Grandpa found a piece of clay and fashioned a little clay boy. He put him by the fire to dry and said to Grandma, "Our children are grown up. They are far away. We'll have a new child now. We won't be alone anymore."

The clay boy dried out by the fire. And suddenly he moved his hands. Then he moved his feet. Then he jumped up and said,

"I am here! I am hungry!"

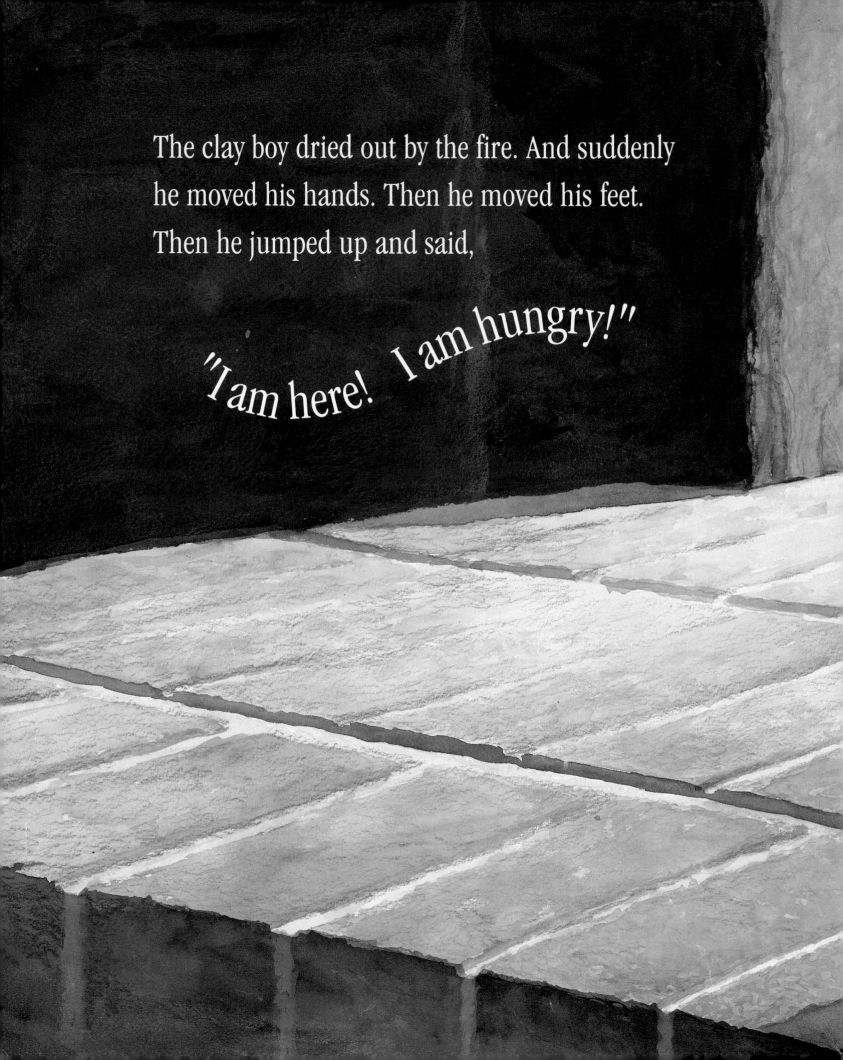

Grandma gave him milk.

Grandpa gave him bread.

In a wink, the clay boy gulped it all down and cried,

" More! I want more!"

He ate and ate. He grew and grew. He ate up all the food in the house and still cried,

So he gulped down the chickens,

and he gulped down the geese,

and the cat,

and the dog.

And he got
bigger,

and bigger,

and bigger.

Then—*gulp!*—he swallowed Grandma.

And—*gulp!*—he swallowed Grandpa.

Then—

thump,
thump,
thump—

he went out of the house on his big clay feet,

and—

thump,
thump,
thump—

he went down the street.

He met two women bringing water from the well.

Gulp! He swallowed them, pails and all.

He met a peasant with a wagon-load of hay.

Gulp!

He swallowed the peasant, and the wagon,
and the horse, and the hay.

Thump, thump, he went.
And—*gulp, gulp!*—

he swallowed everyone he met,
till there was **nobody** left in the village.

And still he cried,

"More! I want more!"

He came out into the field, where a little white goat
with golden eyes was grazing on a hill.

"Ho!" he cried. "I've found more food!
I'll eat you now!"

The little white goat
looked down at the clay boy,
and he said,
"I'm ready.

You can eat me if you wish. But do not trouble
to climb the hill. Just close your eyes, and
open your mouth, and I'll jump right in."

So the clay boy closed his eyes,
and opened his mouth, and waited.
And the little white goat bent down
his head, and aimed his horns,
and took a great, wide leap—

straight
at
the
big
fat
belly.

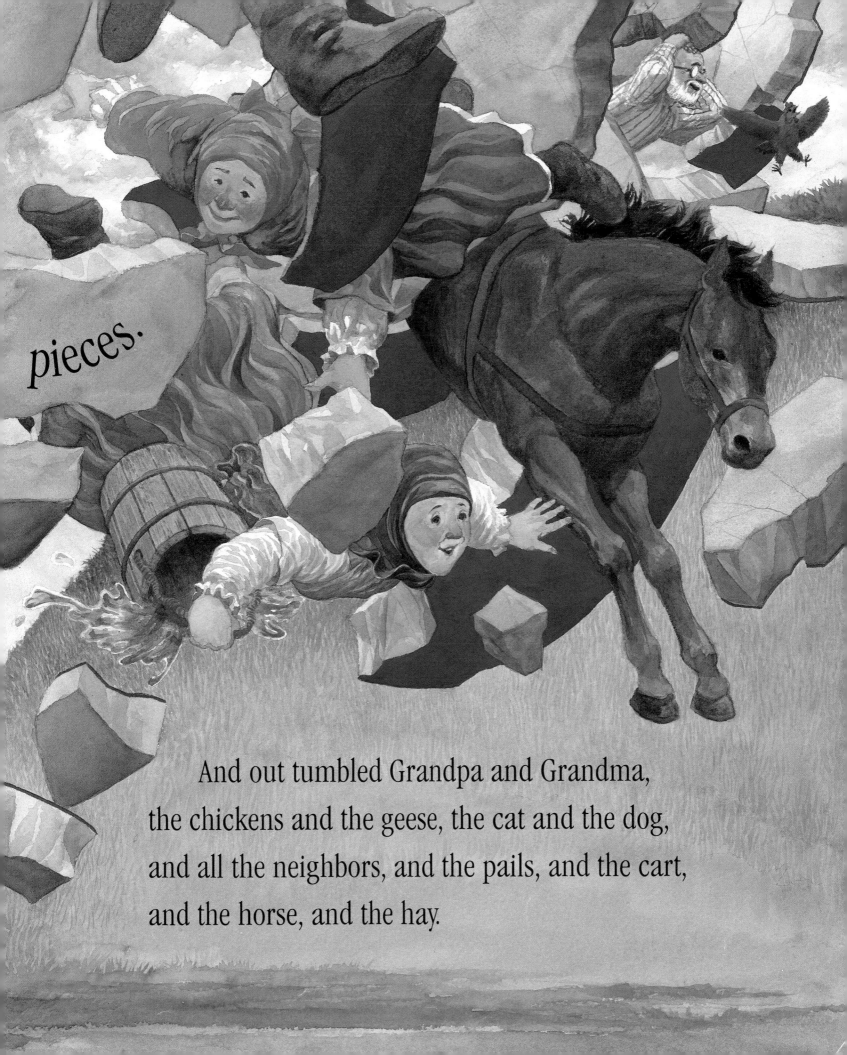

pieces.

And out tumbled Grandpa and Grandma,
the chickens and the geese, the cat and the dog,
and all the neighbors, and the pails, and the cart,
and the horse, and the hay.

Everybody laughed and sang and
danced around the little white goat.
They painted his horns golden
to match his golden eyes.

And they said, "We shall never forget
how the clever little goat saved our
village from the greedy clay boy."

They told the story to their children and their
children's children. I heard it from my grand-
mother, who was a child of a child of a child.
And now that I've told it to you,
it's your turn to tell it
to all who will listen.